PUFFIN BOOKS

ASK ME NO QUESTIONS

Poor Verity! She used to love making up extraordinary stories, excuses for being late or for not finishing her homework. But now she can't open her mouth without speaking the truth, no matter how awkward or unpleasant it might be.

The cause of this change is a bag of special 'truth sweets', which Verity later tries on other people, with some unexpected results – especially for Samson Smirkalott, the town mayor.

This very funny story should provoke some interesting discussion about the merits of absolute honesty. Is is necessarily *always* the best policy?

Clare Bevan was born and brought up in Berkshire, where she still lives with her husband, baby son, and cats. Previously a teacher, Clare has an Open University degree. Her main hobby is amateur dramatics, and she has written many plays, sketches and monologues. Her first novel, *Mightier than the Sword*, won the Kathleen Fidler Award, and is also available in Puffin.

CLARE BEVAN

Ask Me No Questions

Illustrated by Honey de Lacey

PUFFIN BOOKS

Dedicated to my three nieces:
Rachel, Victoria and Candace
with lots of love.

'The truth is rarely pure and never simple.'
Oscar Wilde

PUFFIN BOOKS

Published by the Penguin Group
Penguin Books Ltd, 27 Wrights Lane, London W8 5TZ, England
Penguin Books USA Inc., 375 Hudson Street, New York, New York 10014, USA
Penguin Books Australia Ltd, Ringwood, Victoria, Australia
Penguin Books Canada Ltd, 10 Alcorn Avenue, Toronto, Ontario, Canada M4V 3B2
Penguin Books (NZ) Ltd, 182–190 Wairau Road, Auckland 10, New Zealand

Penguin Books Ltd, Registered Offices: Harmondsworth, Middlesex, England

First published by Blackie and Son Ltd 1991
Published in Puffin Books 1993
10 9 8 7 6 5 4 3 2 1

Text copyright © Clare Bevan, 1991
Illustrations copyright © Honey de Lacey, 1991
All rights reserved

The moral right of the author has been asserted

Printed in England by Clays Ltd, St Ives plc

1 . . . *The Gift*

Verity liked being late for school. It meant she could tell her teacher a really good story. A great, huge, enormous whopper. A gigantic fib.

'Sorry, Miss Proudfoot, but the post van broke down, and I had to help the postman push it all the way up the hill.'

Or, 'A gorilla escaped from the pet shop, and it wouldn't let me go until I bought it a bunch of bananas.'

Or, 'I saw a bank robber running down the road, so I tripped him up with a rugby tackle, and I had to collect a medal from the police station.'

Stuff like that. Little lies were no good. The stories had to be really shocking or nobody would believe them. If Verity tried something feeble like, 'My mum forgot to wake me up,' or, 'I couldn't find my games kit,' her teacher would just frown and say:

'Not good enough, Verity. Extremely disappointing. Stay in and write a hundred lines.'

On this particular morning, Verity walked into

the classroom five minutes after everyone else.

'You're late again,' grumbled Miss Proudfoot. 'What's your excuse this time?'

Verity could hardly wait. 'I was hurrying down the street when a little old lady stopped me. She wanted me to hold her wool while she finished her knitting, and you'll never guess what happened next…'

'Yes, yes,' interrupted Miss Proudfoot with a weary flap of the fingers. She was trying to add up the dinner money, but the sums were giving her a

headache. 'That's quite enough, Verity. Very amusing. Very original. Now off you go to assembly, and leave me in peace.'

Verity smiled as she followed the other children down the corridor to the hall. She had won again. In fact, the knitting story was so good she would probably try it on someone else. Mum perhaps. Tonight.

'Once upon a time,' roared the headmaster from the stage, as soon as the first hymn was over, 'there was a horrible, disgusting, objectionable little girl. And the worst thing about her was that she told lies. All the time. To everybody. And do you know what happened to her?'

The children muttered and fidgeted and stared at their shoes.

'In the end, nobody believed a single word she said,' shouted the headmaster more loudly than ever, 'and as a result, her house caught fire and she was burned to death.'

I bet she wasn't, thought Verity. I bet her teacher gave her a gold star for making up such clever stories.

But the headmaster hadn't finished, even though his face had gone completely purple. 'Then there was a perfectly ghastly little boy who

called out, "Wolf! Wolf!" when there wasn't any wolf about at all. And what do you think became of him?'

I bet he grew up to be a famous actor, thought Verity. I bet he had his own TV show, and a gorgeous house with a heated swimming pool, and…

'He was eaten alive by a flock of angry sheep,' thundered the Headmaster. 'Which jolly well served him right. You should always tell the truth. Pure and simple. Now we shall sing, "All Things Bright and Beautiful"…'

Walking home from school that evening, Verity stared hard at the ground. She was trying to think of a really good fib to tell her family if they asked her what she had been doing in class today.

'We tied Miss Proudfoot to a tree in the playground. Then we did a war-dance round her for our American Indians project.'

Or, 'We all played football on the roof because the workmen came to mow the games field.'

Or…

'Excuse me, little girl,' said a voice that crackled like an empty crisp packet. 'Could you help me with my wool? I was doing my knitting, and I

appear to have dropped a stitch.'

Verity blinked. She rubbed her eyes. Sitting on the iron bench outside the post office was the strangest, most shrivelled-up old lady she had ever seen. Bother, she thought. This is just like my story. Now I shan't be able to use it again because I hate telling the truth. It's so boring.

'Hold this for me,' croaked the thin, whiskery mouth, and Verity found herself sitting on the bench with a tickly tangle of black wool wrapped round her fingers.

'It's best bat's fleece,' explained the old lady. 'If you wear a hat made out of that, you won't keep bumping into lampposts all the time.'

'But I don't bump into lampposts,' Verity began. 'I…'

The old lady let out a needle-sharp screech and pounced at the crack in a paving slab. 'There you are, you saucy little skally-diddle,' she cried, holding up an invisible something in front of Verity's nose.

'I can't see anything,' said Verity. 'What is it? A sneeze? A hole? A breath of fresh air?'

'It's my dropped stitch, of course,' cackled the old lady triumphantly. Her bony fingers were already knitting furiously, casting off the last row of what appeared to be a large black dish-cloth.

'Finished,' she cried, snatching the spare wool from Verity's thumbs and skewering the bundle with a pair of porcupine quills. 'Now, let's have a look at the map.'

With that, she spread out the dish-cloth across her knobbly knees, and stabbed it with a fingernail so sharp it could have sunk an ocean-liner. 'Straight past the Saturn flyover, over the Titan roundabout, then first left after Venus,' she muttered to herself anxiously. 'Where did you say I was?'

'I didn't,' said Verity. 'I don't think you asked me.'

The old lady swivelled round and stared at her like an ancient sparrow. 'This is Planet Y-Not, isn't it?'

'Well.' Verity's throat felt dry, and she wiggled her fingers under her collar. 'Not exactly. This is…'

'Oh botheration. Now I'll never get there in time, and I do so hate being late.' The old lady pulled up her sleeve and tapped at the face of her wrist-watch.

The watch glared back at her and waved its twelve hairy legs angrily. 'I'm doing my best, you know,' it squeaked. 'It's not my fault you keep jumping through time-warps and forgetting to wind me up.'

'Well, I'm winding you up now, aren't I?' snapped the old lady. 'What year are we in, according to the new Galactic Universal Calendar?'

'Thirty-three squillion and two,' squeaked the watch. 'And it's past my lunch-break, as a matter of fact.'

The old lady fed it a luminous bug, then covered it with her cuff and groaned. 'I've missed the

ceremony,' she told Verity. 'I've taken a wrong turning through the asteroid belt, and now I'm going to be sixty years too late. It's my own fault. I should never have trusted this "Do-It-Yourself" Map Kit.' She threw the black dishcloth on the floor and stamped on it with her spiky heels.

'Late, did you say?' Verity sat up, interested. 'Does it matter? Can't you make up an excuse? I know some really good ones...'

'Of course not.' The old lady screamed so loudly that a passing burglar dropped his bag of bank-notes and ran into the police station for safety. 'I'm supposed to be at a Royal Christening Party, you infuriating little specimen. If I turn up now, all the guests will have gone home, and the baby will be nearly as old as I am. And I bet there won't be a crumb of cake left with any icing on it. What am I going to do?'

'Go home?' suggested Verity, realising that she was rather late herself by now. She stood up and hitched her school bag on her shoulder, ready to set off down the road.

'But I have to deliver my Christening Gift,' protested the old lady. 'I can't take it back to the enchantment store. That's supposed to be terribly bad luck, and in any case I've lost my receipt.'

She pulled a small, crumpled package from a pocket concealed in the hem of her skirt. The wrappings were as dull and wrinkled as her own skin, but the label was a shimmering star that changed colour every time it caught the light.

'Oh,' gasped Verity, automatically reaching out her hand. Then she remembered all the lessons she had been taught about strangers, and stepped backwards again, squashing the toe of a passing postman.

'Sorry,' he said. 'It's not been my day.' And he

clambered into his van clutching a remarkably empty sack. The engine coughed twice then stopped.

'I know,' said Verity to the old lady. 'Why don't you put your parcel in the post-box? Then you can blame the postman if anyone complains.'

'Thanks very much,' came a dismal voice from underneath the bonnet of the post van. 'That's all I need. I don't know why everyone has to be so rude about the postal service. I don't really.' And he began to push his van slowly away up the hill. EVEN OUR SECOND CLASS IS FIRST CLASS, said the slogan on the back of his uniform.

'No. I don't think I'll bother with the post,' said the old lady. 'In any case, I can't afford the price of a stamp to the outermost edge of the Galaxy.'

She held out the little parcel and made it rattle. It sounded like chocolate drops or peppermints or chunks of seaside rock, and Verity's mouth started to water. She took another step backwards, colliding with the pillar-box this time. It grinned at her painfully.

'No thanks. Sorry,' she tried to explain. 'But my mum says I'm not allowed to take sweets from strangers. And you're the strangest person I've ever met...'

15

'That's as may be,' the old lady agreed. 'Except these aren't ordinary sweets. They're a Christening Gift for a very special little girl.' She looked at her watch again, and it waved back at her hungrily. 'Must go,' she added. 'It's feeding time. Can't stop to argue.'

She pushed the parcel into the top of Verity's schoolbag, then muttered a string of peculiar words that sounded inside out and upside down. 'Goodbye, Verity,' she called, holding on to her dented hat with both hands. 'A long life and a fizzy one.' Her whole body was beginning to wobble and lose its colour, like a worn-out video picture.

'Hey! Wait!' Verity shouted back. 'How did you know my name?'

'How do you think?' The voice came from a faint, rippling cloud that hovered above the iron bench. 'It's written on your Christening Present...' Then the sound faded away too, and the old lady vanished.

Verity shrugged. OK. Fine. If that was the way things were. She looked round to see if anyone else had noticed an old woman disappearing in a puff of green dust, but the only other person on the pavement was the man from the pet shop. He was holding a baby gorilla by the hand, and was too

busy feeding it bananas to bother about anything else.

Verity tucked her school bag under her arm and began to run as fast as she could in the opposite direction. She was going to be in big trouble when she got home.

'Where have you been?' grumbled Mum when Verity burst into the living-room. 'I've been worried sick.' She popped a sugared almond between her teeth and turned the page of her *True Love* magazine.

'Sorry, Mum. But I had to push the post van up the hill, and…'

Mum's eyebrows quivered dangerously.

'There was an escaped gorilla, and…'

Mum made a little gargling noise in the back of her throat.

'I captured a bank robber, and…'

Mum exploded. Sugared almonds bounced off her lap and rolled round the carpet. 'How many times have I warned you about all these lies? I can always tell, you know. Now, the truth please. And no more stories.'

Verity shrugged. 'OK,' she said. 'I met this weird old lady with a talking watch, and she made me hold her knitting while she looked for a dropped stitch. And she found it on the pavement. And she gave me a christening present. And then she just dis…'

'Verity!'

Mum threw her magazine on the floor, pushed a teacup to one side, and jammed her feet into a pair of fluffy slippers. Always a dangerous sign.

'If I've told you once, I've told you a thousand times. Little girls who tell lies get spots on their tongues. Now, up to your room without any tea. And I don't want to hear another word from you all evening.'

Verity opened her mouth to protest. After all, she had real proof, didn't she? Her christening present in its crinkled paper. She reached her hand into the top of her bag. 'But, Mum…'

Her mother made another gargling noise and almost stood up.

Verity took the hint.

Upstairs in her bedroom she stamped up and down the bed, and kicked her pyjamas at the door. 'Typical,' she muttered. 'Absolutely typical. Grown-ups are so stupid. If you tell them the truth, they never believe you.'

Of course she knew that was partly because she was always telling lies. Of course she knew she was a bit like the boy who cried, 'Wolf!' A lot like him, actually. But all the same…

'If that's how Mum feels, I'll never tell the truth again. Why should I? There's no point.' And she crash-landed on the duvet in a haze of fluff and bad temper. What was she going to do with herself? How was she going to spend the long hours till bedtime?

She knew there was a long list of homework in her schoolbag. Maths and Topic and English and Science. If she wanted, she could give Miss Proudfoot a really nice surprise in the morning. But she didn't want to.

She snatched up a copy of the *Boppo* comic from her bedside table, and turned the pages crossly. All the cartoon children had fat, cheeky faces, and they were always playing clever tricks on their grown-ups. Mums and dads skidded downstairs on stray roller skates. Teachers got their feet stuck in buckets of glue. Policemen's helmets fell on hamsters and ran away.

'All stories,' Verity said to herself. 'Real life isn't like that. The grown-ups win every time.'

She was feeling hungry now. Rumbly and grumbly and ready for a toasted cheese sandwich. She collapsed on her pillow and counted the cracks in the ceiling. Ninety-one, ninety-two…

The door opened and her big brother leapt in, doing his Super Hero impression. This was a waste of time, because he had pimples on his chin and his best jumper had shrunk in the wash. He looked more like Wimp Man from the back of the *Boppo* comic.

'How do I look?' he asked, twirling round and slicking back his hair with a wet finger. 'Pretty cool, huh?' The strand flopped back over his forehead and dangled in his eye.

Pretty pathetic, thought Verity. He looks like something Mum found when she was washing the cabbages.

'Incredible,' she said. 'Really unbelievable. Where are you going?'

Bill winked at her, which was quite an operation, as it involved holding down one eyelid while the other one flapped about trying to stay open.

'Out with the boys,' he shouted in an extra loud voice for Mum to hear. 'Down to the skating rink for a couple of hours. Pretty boring, I expect.' But his lips carried on moving when the sound ran out. 'Jaaaay,' they seemed to be saying. 'Neeee.'

Verity nodded. She understood. He was going to meet Janey Sullivan, the girl who sat in the box office at the ice rink. She always wore purple, and her hair was plaited with strings of shiny beads. Mum didn't like her.

'Lucky old you,' whispered Verity. 'I've got to stay here all evening. Just because I told Mum a tiny little story.'

'Well, it's your own fault,' said Bill, admiring himself in the mirror. 'You shouldn't tell so many lies.'

'But I didn't,' Verity tried to explain. 'It was all true. I met this old lady with a talking watch, and she…'

'Sorry,' said Bill. 'Got to go. Can't keep the boys waiting, can I?' And he winked again, looking more like Wimp Man than ever.

When he had gone, Verity threw her pillow at the door. She was hungry, that was the trouble. She should have been tucking into a plate of scrambled eggs by now, or baked potatoes, or beefburgers, or…

She looked around the room. There was a biscuit tin next to her bed, but there was nothing inside it apart from a few crumbs and her tame woodlouse. She felt in her pockets. Nothing. Some out-of-date raffle tickets for a trip to Disneyland, a drawing-pin she had found in her shoe, a button off someone else's shirt, a rubber band and a miniature harmonica. She stuck it in her mouth. Blow. Suck. Blow. Suck. Useless. It sounded like a dying cat.

She was left with two options. Either she could go and eat a tubeful of toothpaste in the bathroom. Or...

She looked at her schoolbag. Why not? The present had been given to her, and she had earned it by being friendly to the old lady, just like the heroes in famous fairy stories. Her fingers tingled and her tummy rumbled again. She opened her bag, closed her eyes, and reached inside.

The parcel was shaped like a lop-sided box with a bulging lid, and she squeezed it gently as she twisted it over and over. What could it be? A magic potion for making her rich and beautiful? A secret recipe that would turn her into a giant? A medicine to give her a brain like a computer?

She opened her eyes and peered at the label. The star was pale mauve now, but deep inside it something jiggled like a tiny black insect. She squinted closer and made out a single, wriggling word. Verity. Her own name, just as the old lady had said.

Verity shrugged, which was the best way to deal with impossible problems. She unpinned the star and tucked it back into her bag. Then she tore off the paper and scrunched it between her hands. It was as cold as a snowball, and when she unfolded her fingers all that remained was a blob of ice which melted and dripped on the duvet.

She was left with the gift itself. A lop-sided box with a bulgy lid. She lifted one corner cautiously, half expecting a rubber snake to leap out, or a giggling demon with hairy ears.

It was all very disappointing really. No flashing lights. No explosions. No coils of green smoke or unearthly smells. Not even a genie. Just a bag of brown cloth, tied up with a pink ribbon.

Stitched across each side was an embroidered message. On the front was an old saying, 'The Truth Is Rarely Pure And Never Simple'. On the back was something that either said, 'Caution' or 'Carry On', but wouldn't stay still long enough for Verity to make up her mind. So she shrugged again and untied the pink ribbon.

'Boring,' she grumbled. It was just a bag of sweets after all. She might have known. But why do strangers always offer you sweets? And why shouldn't you eat them? Mum said it was because the sweets were a sort of bait, like worms on a fishing rod, only not quite so slimy.

'Well, the old lady can't catch me now, can she? Because she's already disappeared,' Verity argued to herself. 'So one little sweet can't do any harm, can it? Not if I clean my teeth afterwards.'

In any case, she was extremely hungry. Hungrier every minute. So if anything awful happened to her, it would all be Mum's fault.

'I hope I turn into a frog, or grow a nose like a carrot. Then she'll be sorry,' said Verity, licking her lips.

She dipped into the bag and drew out a glistening blue lozenge. It had silver stripes inside it that rippled like waves, and little golden lights that flickered on and off. She sniffed it to make sure. It didn't smell poisonous. Not that she knew how poison ought to smell, but she guessed it must be something like mouldy socks or burnt rice pudding.

She opened her mouth, dropped the sweet on her tongue, and waited for something strange to happen. Would she shrink, or feel sick, or start to grow fur?

The sweet seemed to uncoil between her teeth and wrap itself round her tongue. Then it slithered past her tonsils and trickled down her throat, leaving behind a taste that was sugary and sharp and tickly and smooth all at once.

'Scrummy,' said Verity, licking her lips again. She was tempted to try another, but she noticed that the bag had retied itself and was sitting back inside its box as if to say, 'Enough is as good as a feast'.

In fact, she felt quite full already, and there was a peculiar fizzing sensation in her stomach which took her mind off feeling hungry. She crept across to the mirror, half expecting to see a monster with three eyes, or a puppet with painted hair, but she looked just the same as usual. She was so cross, she stuck out her tongue. It looked slightly blue, and it was covered in gold and silver spots. That was all.

'So much for magic,' she said moodily. 'And I thought this was going to be my lucky day.'

She wandered over to her writing desk and took out her secret notebook from its hiding place inside *One Thousand And One Amazing True Facts For Girls And Boys*. Next, she found her favourite felt-pen and turned to her special 'Good Excuses' page. She put crosses next to 'Escaped Gorilla', 'Bank Robber' and 'Post Van', to remind herself not to use them again for at least three weeks. Then she put a tick and two crosses next to 'Old Lady Knitting', to show that it had worked but was no good any more.

Finally, she wrote the following day's date in the

margin and chewed her pen thoughtfully. Miss Proudfoot had given everyone a Maths card for homework, but Verity had left hers at school. Accidentally on purpose. So she was going to need a good story to help her out of trouble.

Not, 'My new puppy was sick in my schoolbag,' because she had tried that one before, and Emily Forthright had ruined it by saying, 'But your mum won't let you have any pets, will she? In case they leave fluff on the furniture.'

Verity nibbled the top off her pen.

Not, 'My poor old granny caught the mumps and I had to take her a bunch of grapes,' because Miss Proudfoot lived next door to Gran and was bound to notice if she didn't have a bulgy face.

Verity rolled her pen down the lid of the desk. This was hopeless. It would have been quicker to do the stupid homework. Less effort, anyway. She picked up the pen and began to write, 'I had an awful nose-bleed all over my maths book so Mum made me throw it away'.

At least, that was what she had intended to say, but when her hand stopped scribbling she looked at the page in horror. 'I didn't do my work,' it read, 'because I just couldn't be bothered.'

'But I can't say that,' Verity hissed at the

notebook. 'Miss Proudfoot would have a thousand fits. She'd string me up by the ears and eat me for dinner. I can't possibly…' Her stomach fizzed, and once more she seemed to feel the silver waves ripple around her tongue. She tried again.

'My mum thought the work card was an advert for Double Glazing, so she put it in the waste disposal, and it got chewed into a billion pieces,' she began. But as soon as she finished, the words danced about along the lines until the story said, 'I was feeling so lazy, I left the card at school and

I didn't do my work because I just couldn't be both-ered

read my *Boppo* comic instead'.

'No, no, no!' Verity ripped the page out of her notebook, screwed it up into a tight wodge, and jumped on it. 'I never, never, never tell the…'

Fizz, tingle, ripple.

She looked in the mirror. Was it just her imagination, or had her tongue turned even bluer than before? And were there really more gold and silver spots this time?

'Verity!' It was Mum's voice calling from the hall. 'Gran's here to see you, so you'd better come and say hello. But don't you dare tell her any of your stories, or else…'

Good old Gran. Verity hid her notebook back inside *One Thousand And One Amazing True Facts For Boys And Girls*, and skidded down the stairs. She hoped no one would notice her blue tongue. Or her sparkling spots.

'Hello, Gran,' she said cheerfully. 'You look ever so old tonight. You've got lots of floppy wrinkles under your eyes and a whisker on your chin.'

'Verity!' Mum was so angry, she turned down the sound on her TV programme. It was a court-room drama, and the judge stared out of the screen, opening and shutting his lips in silent

33

astonishment.

'Sorry,' said Verity. 'I was only telling the truth, like you told me. The truth, the whole truth, and nothing but the truth. Are you staying for supper, Gran? Have you brought us something nice to eat?'

'Hm,' said Gran, clicking her false teeth. 'What you need is Good Manners Soup and Best Behaviour Pie. And double helpings too.' She tied an apron over her coat and pottered out into the kitchen with her carrier bag. It smelt of apples and spicy buns. Verity followed her.

'I'd offer to help,' she said honestly, 'but I don't feel like it at the moment. Sorry.' This was getting very embarrassing. She couldn't stop telling the truth, and the words were tumbling out all by themselves.

Luckily, Gran was making such a clatter with the spoons and saucepans that she couldn't hear a thing, so Verity hurried back to the living-room and plonked herself on the settee beside her mum.

'That programme's rubbish,' she said almost at once. 'Miss Proudfoot says you need a brain the size of a baked bean to watch it.'

Her mum began to make gargling noises, but

Verity couldn't stop. She was flicking through Mum's copy of *True Love* magazine now.

'People make all these stories up, you know,' she announced loudly. 'Most of them are written by the editor, only he pretends he's someone else. Amelia Teardrop or Daphne Dearheart. Soppy names like that.'

Mum made a grab for *True Love*, but she was too late. Verity was already reading out the start of 'This Week's Star Story'.

'Gerald ran his fingers through Melissa's golden curls. "Oh, Gerald," she murmured blissfully. "How handsome you are."' Verity shut the magazine and grinned at her mother.

'See,' she said triumphantly. 'It's daft. Melissa wouldn't murmur anything like that. She'd stamp on his foot and she'd say, "Stop messing about, you fool. This hair-do cost me a fortune." Wouldn't she?'

Mum's face went tight and slightly crooked. She took the magazine, folded it in half, and stuffed it into the litter-bin. 'I'll have to cancel my order now,' she wailed. 'You've spoiled my fun, you horrible child.'

'Supper's ready,' cooed Gran round the doorway. 'Fresh apple scones. Come and eat them

while they're hot.'

Verity didn't wait to be asked twice. She charged into the kitchen before Mum could stop her, and sank her teeth into a steaming goody. 'More like rock cakes, Gran,' she said, licking the butter off her fingers. 'Hard as concrete, but I don't mind. I'm starving.'

She knew it was the wrong thing to say. She knew she was asking for trouble again. But there was nothing she could do about it. She just couldn't help telling the truth.

She scraped the hard left-over crumbs into a neat pile on the edge of her plate, not daring to look up. She didn't want to see Gran's eyes go all watery, or watch Mum's face tighten into a frown, so she counted to ten and waited for their tempers to erupt. Seven, eight, nine, nine-and-a-half, nine-and-three-quarters...

She looked up. Mum and Gran were sorting through a bagful of rustling tissue paper, and were so busy chatting that they seemed to have forgotten about Verity altogether.

'Hm, hm,' she coughed. 'Can I have another scone, Gran? Please?'

Gran beamed. 'Of course you can,' she said. 'Nice to see you've found your manners. I expect you were just hungry.' She pottered across to her cake tin and chose a very large and lumpy scone for Verity's plate. 'Now, tell me,' she added. 'What did you do at school today?'

Same old question every time. Verity swallowed a mouthful of burnt currants while she decided on tonight's story. Should it be the one about Miss Proudfoot being chased down the corridor by the class gerbil, and getting her foot stuck in the caretaker's bucket? Or the one about the headmaster riding to school in a helicopter to beat the traffic jams? Or...

She opened her mouth, ready for a bit of fun. Gran quite liked being teased, so it really didn't matter. 'Actually, we watched a TV programme about electricity, and then we had to build a model lighthouse. Only mine wouldn't work because I forgot to stick the wires to the bulb, so Miss Proudfoot tried to help me and she got an electric shock. That's all,' she heard herself say. This was awful. Terrible. Unbelievable. Every single boring word was true.

Gran giggled, spilling crumbs down her front. 'Oh, Verity. You are a one. You and your tall stories. I never know...'

'But it's not a story, Gran. It's the truth. Honestly.

You ask Miss…'

'Verity!' Mum was looking dangerous again, and her face was tighter than ever. 'Perhaps you'd like to do the washing-up for your gran?'

'No I wouldn't,' said Verity before she had time to stop herself. 'I hate washing-up.' She knew before she had finished that this was a bad move.

'How dare you?' Mum was spluttering. 'I don't know what's got into you this evening, I really don't.'

'Sorry, Mum.' Verity was pretty confused herself. What had got into her? Two rock buns, and one blue lozenge… 'I was just telling the truth, you see. I don't like washing-up. Nobody does.' This still wasn't helping matters. She began again. 'But of course I'll do it, because I like helping Gran.'

She jumped up and began piling the plates in the sink. Then she ran a bowl of frothy water and played with it while the grown-ups gossiped. She listened with half an ear as she hummed to herself and dabbled around with a plastic brush.

'I've bought myself a new hat,' Gran was saying. 'I found it in the sales. And that nosy Mrs Grummet was ever so jealous. She says it makes me look a different woman.'

She rustled around in the tissue paper some

more, then pulled something pink and spiky out of a paper bag. 'How do I look?' she asked proudly, perching the creation over one eye.

'Oh, yes,' exclaimed Mum. 'Very original. Very different. I can see what Mrs Grummet means.'

'It's different all right,' said Verity. 'You look like a hedgehog with a headache. Or a punk porcupine. Or a frightened blancmange. If you walk down the street wearing that, you'll make everyone cry with laughing. No wonder it was in the sale. I bet they've been trying to sell it for about

40

a hundred years.'

She splashed a soapy hand across her mouth to stop herself, but it was no good. Now the words had escaped, they could never be unsaid. Gran would probably cry, and Mum would go crazy. No tea for a week. No treats. No television.

'I'm sorry,' she whimpered. 'I can't help it. It's not my fault. Everyone keeps telling me to tell the truth, and now…'

Silence. Not even the rustling of torn tissue.

She wheeled round, her face covered in bubbles. Mum and Gran had gone. They must have rushed upstairs straightaway to admire Gran's hat in the wardrobe mirror.

Verity dried her hands and took herself off to the living-room, where she collapsed on the settee and stared at the blank television screen. Things were beginning to get out of hand, she decided. In fact, if she opened her mouth once more this evening, she had a nasty feeling she was going to put her foot in it.

Gran had left her copy of the local paper on the coffee table, so Verity twisted it round to look at the front page. 'Shopping Trolley Found On The Moon', blared the main headline. 'Pop Star Ate My Prize Rubber Plant'.

I don't believe a word of it, she thought. Why do people bother to read this stuff? Don't they realise it's all nonsense?

She picked up the zapper to switch on the television, then leaned back with her hands over her mouth, just in case.

'Try our new Chocky Chomp bars,' said a plummy voice, as a tired mermaid munched into a flaky snack. Immediately a giant fish swam to the surface, and the mermaid gave him a chunk as well. Then they both swam away into the sunset together, while the plummy voice sang, 'Chocky Chomp's so good for you … Lots of fun for your best friend too.'

'Oh no it's not,' Verity's tongue tried to say, as she reached for the off switch. 'It gives you spots and makes your teeth fall out.' But the sound that escaped through her fingers sounded more like, 'Oh do ids dot.'

'What were you saying, dear?' Gran had just walked in, still wearing her ridiculous hat. She sat down at the other end of the settee looking pleased with herself.

Verity just shook her head. She didn't want to say anything at all. She pressed harder on her lips, and attempted to smile at Gran by waggling her eyebrows instead.

'Are you feeling all right, lovey? You're not sickening for something are you?'

Nod nod. Shake shake. Please don't let me say anything rude about Gran's hat, thought Verity. Please don't let me ruin her day.

Slowly she unpeeled her fingers, and before anything worse could happen she said, 'Gran...is it always best to tell the truth?'

'Of course,' said Gran happily, leaning back so that her hat slipped over her nose. 'That's what I was told, anyway. And I see no reason to change my mind now.'

'In that case...' Verity tried very hard not to look at the spiky pink blob. 'Why do you buy such a silly newspaper? And why did you tell me all

43

those stories about Father Christmas and the Tooth Fairy?'

'For goodness' sake, stop pestering.' Mum had come in with a bottle of nail varnish and a large tube of wine-gums. 'Ask me no questions, and I'll tell you no lies. Isn't that right, Gran?'

Gran nodded. The pink blob wobbled. 'That's what people always used to say,' she agreed.

On went the television again, and they all squashed together on the settee, sucking their sweets noisily and making rude remarks about the news-readers.

'Why does she always wear those dangly ear-rings? They make me feel dizzy.'

'Did you know he keeps a pet llama in his back garden? Unhygienic I call it, and so does Mrs Grummet.'

'These wine-gums aren't made from real wine, you know. It's just flavouring. There ought to be a great big warning on the packet...'

'Ssssh,' said Mum and Gran at once, pointing at the news-girl. 'She's getting to the interesting bit. You can always tell.'

The reporter was shuffling a large bunch of papers importantly, and peering over the top of her glasses. 'And now,' she said, 'Mr Samson Smirkalot. Local businessman and Town Mayor ...Tell me, Mr Smirkalot. Is it true that you are planning to demolish the entire village and build a giant car-park over the children's playground?'

The Mayor twirled his bow tie and gave the camera a sickly smile. Then he rubbed the side of his nose. 'Ah. Well,' he began. His voice sounded as if he had been gargling with olive oil. 'I wouldn't say demolished exactly. I prefer to talk about redevelopment. Vast improvements. Exciting new designs. Progress.'

The news-reader shuffled her papers even more

importantly than before. 'But what about the village shops? And the post office? And the school? How can we be sure…?'

'Ah. Yes. Well.' The Mayor gave his nose an extra thorough rub. 'One or two buildings may have to be temporarily dismantled, of course. But I can assure you it's all in the very best interests of the general public. You see…'

Here he held up a photograph of an extremely large car. It had 'Mayor 1' printed on the number plate, and there was a tiny statue of Mr Smirkalot on the bonnet. 'What people really need these days…'

'Why doesn't he just tell the truth?' demanded Verity. 'Why doesn't he say he's going to do whatever he likes, because he wants to make a lot of money for himself?'

'Oh,' said Mum. 'That's obvious. If he admitted that, no one would vote for him again, would they?'

Someone came thumping in at the front door, and Verity could tell from the off-key whistling that it was Bill. She wondered if he had enjoyed his evening with Janey Sullivan.

'Hi, Mum. Hi, Gran. Hi, Vee,' he called. He sounded unusually cheerful.

'Come and give your old gran a kiss,' Gran shouted back, and Bill crashed in with a grin all over his face.

'Had a nice time with the boys?' asked Mum, offering him a wine-gum. 'What have you been doing?'

'Oh. You know,' said Bill, giving Gran a hug. 'Had a few races with Chas and Jim. And I won.'

Please don't let me say anything I'm going to regret, thought Verity. Her mouth opened all by itself, but she snatched the wine-gums out of Mum's hand and jammed a black square between her teeth. Ask me no questions. Please. Ask me no questions.

'And what do you think of Gran's nice new hat?' asked Mum, snatching the wine-gums back and giving Verity a nasty look.

'Lovely,' said Bill with his mouth full. 'Very classy, Gran…Makes her look a different woman, doesn't it, Vee?'

'Urrrgggh,' Verity mumbled desperately. But it was hopeless. Her tongue couldn't wait to take over, and there was nothing she could do to stop it. 'If you ask me, Gran's hat looks like an exploding jellyfish, and we ought to tell her before she makes a complete fool of herself. And Bill hasn't been skating. He's been kissing Janey Sullivan. That's why he's got purple smudges all over his chin.'

The room fell silent. Only the news-reader spoke.

'Thank you so much, Mr Smirkalot. I'm sure you've put all our minds at rest. It's good to know that there are still people like you in the world, and that our little village will remain totally unspoiled for many years to come.'

The Mayor rubbed his nose, and smiled more broadly than ever.

That night, Verity dreamt.

She walked down the street and saw newspaper hoardings that read, 'Nothing Interesting Happened Today And Nobody Did Anything Exciting At All'.

Or, 'Town Mayor Tells Terrible Fibs On Television'.

Or, 'News-Reporter Sacked For Making Up Naughty Stories About Famous People'.

She heard Gran talking to Mrs Grummet.

Gran said, 'You're a nosy old busybody, and you really get on my nerves.'

Mrs Grummet said, 'You shouldn't have bought that stupid hat. It makes you look like a petrified parrot.'

'Silly old fool,' said Gran.

'Daft old bat,' said Mrs Grummet.

Then they linked arms and went off to the shops, arguing all the way.

Verity wandered home and switched on the television. Six children with completely black teeth

danced across the screen.

'Chocky Chomps are bad for you...They rot your teeth and taste like glue,' they sang merrily.

A woman held up a gleaming white towel and glowered out of the screen. 'Whizzo-Bright made my wash shiny white,' she grumbled. 'Which is worse than you think. It's supposed to be pink.'

'It made mine shrink,' agreed her friend, angrily waving a tiny shirt at the camera. 'And it's so full of holes, it's only fit for moles.'

The alarm rang, and Verity woke up.

The first thing she did was to run to the mirror

to inspect her tongue. It seemed all right. Completely back to normal. No blue blobs, no silver speckles, nothing unusual at all.

'I'm a banana,' she said, just to make sure she wasn't telling the truth any more. 'I've got green hair and my name is Millicent Moneybags.'

Thank goodness for that, she thought. I think it's worn off. I'll go and try it out on Mum.

She dressed quickly and charged downstairs.

'There's a frog in the sink,' she announced as soon as she reached the kitchen. 'It's playing with the plug, and it says it's a royal prince from a country called Bubbles.'

No one answered. Bill spooned up his porridge fiercely while Mum turned up the radio extra loud.

'Miss Proudfoot's going to teach us how to juggle today, so we've all got to take three oranges to school.'

No reply. Verity sat down at the breakfast bar and happily buttered a slice of cold toast. Hooray. She was fine. Totally cured. 'I don't see why everyone was in such a bad mood last night,' she said through a spray of crumbs. 'I was being honest, that's all. And there was no need for Gran to storm off home like that. I was only trying to do

her a favour.'

Mum and Bill picked up their trays and stalked out of the kitchen.

'Mad,' said Verity to herself. 'You just can't please some people.'

She arrived at school before the bell for once, but it didn't matter too much because she was all prepared with a perfect homework excuse for Miss Proudfoot.

'My brother's so shortsighted, he tied my Maths Card on his motorbike by mistake. He thought it was an 'L' plate, you see. So of course…'

'Of course,' groaned Miss Proudfoot. Her head was throbbing more painfully than ever this morning. A visitor was coming to the school. A very important visitor. And she was sure her classroom would never be tidy in time.

'Forget about Maths,' she called out nervously. 'Just empty all the fluff and rubbish out of your desks. We have to look respectable for the photographers. And the reporters. And…' She paused in order to take a deep gulp. '…Mr Samson Smirkalot. Our very own Town Mayor.'

She waited for the children to gasp with surprise and excitement. Half of them stared at her blankly. Ten of them pulled rude faces. Emily Forthright said, 'My dad says old Smirkalot is a crafty windbag.' And all the others carried on playing 'Snap' in the nature corner.

'Well, I want you to be on your very best behaviour this afternoon,' Miss Proudfoot went on, with a little tremble in her voice. 'No giggling. No messing about with paper aeroplanes. No arguing. And no eating. Is that clear?'

Everyone nodded. The 'Snap' players stopped shouting and started whispering, which was helpful of them. Even Emily Forthright promised not to make any clever remarks.

Verity spent the next hour organising her desk. It was incredible how long she could make a simple task last if she wanted to avoid any proper work.

Still, the results were certainly impressive. Every book was stacked neatly and marked with colour-coded sticky paper. Red for Maths, Green for Science, Yellow for English and so on. Her pens were lined up in order of size, her ruler was polished, and every pencil had been sharpened until it could have made holes in a frozen beefburger.

'Very nice indeed,' admitted Miss Proudfoot suspiciously. 'But what have you got inside that peculiar looking box with the lopsided lid? Not sweets, I hope.'

Verity was always chewing in class. And she always said, 'It's a cough drop, miss.' Or, 'It's an indigestion tablet.' Or, 'It's a really yucky pill the doctor gave me for my sore toe.'

Today, she sounded strangely unsure of herself. 'Oh no, miss. It's not sweets. It's a late christening present from an old lady I know. She's got a watch that eats dried beetles.'

'Hm.' Miss Proudfoot narrowed her eyes and

tapped one shoe on the floor. Her left eyelid began to twitch all by itself. She wasn't at all convinced.

She moved away slowly, and pulled an enormous book from the shelf over her table. 'All right, class. Topic folders out. This lesson we're going to start looking at the history of our families, and we'll begin by doing some research on our own names.'

She drew herself up and simpered. 'Of course, you can all imagine what "Proudfoot" means. But what about Peter and Jake and Donna? What do these words tell us about ourselves and about our ancestors?'

She opened the fat book with such a crash that the card players paused in the middle of their game. Peter and Jake and Donna hadn't been interested in a single lesson all term, but this was something new.

'Dunno, miss,' said Jake in his croaky voice. It had got that way from playing 'Snap' every day since last Christmas. 'What do our names mean then?'

Miss Proudfoot perched on her table excitedly and ran her finger down page after page of long lists. 'Peter – A rock, steady and reliable…Jake – See Jack or Jacob…Donna – A precious gift…'

'Miss, miss!'

What was this? A question from Verity of all people? Wonders would never cease. Miss Proudfoot nodded encouragingly, and Verity leaned forwards across her desk lid.

Underneath her hands, underneath the chipped, grimy wood, sat her gift, with its soft pink ribbon and its shimmering label. 'What does "Verity" mean?' she asked. 'Have you got my name in your book?'

Miss Proudfoot flipped the pages with a dampened thumb until she found the back of the girls' section. 'Violet, Victoria, Vesta, Velma,' she muttered. 'Ah. Here we are…Verity – The truth teller…Isn't that lovely!'

'Mmm. Thanks,' began Verity, but her words tailed off and she stared round the room. Everyone was laughing at her. The card players in the corner, the quiet crowd at the front, the noisy bunch by the door, the dreamers in the back row. Everyone.

She felt her face grow warm and she wriggled in her seat. What was so funny? Did she have a smudge of ink on her nose? Was she wearing an odd pair of socks?

'You! The truth teller!' shrieked Emily

Forthright. 'That's the best thing I've heard all year. Just wait till my dad hears about this. He reckons you're an even bigger fibber than Mayor Smirkalot, and that's really saying something.'

Verity frowned. What a cheek. Fancy comparing her with that horrible man in the bow tie. She rubbed the side of her nose. 'I don't tell fibs,' she said weakly. 'I just tell a few stories now and then. What's wrong with that?' But her protests were drowned in another outburst of knee-slapping and desk-thumping.

'All right, everybody. Calm down. Please.' Miss Proudfoot stamped her shoes on the ground until her heels made round dents in the floorboards. 'And let that be a lesson to you, Verity,' she added when the noise had died down, and the rest of the children were mopping their eyes with their sleeves. 'You should always tell the truth. It's much better in the long run.'

'But,' Verity tried to interrupt. 'Not always...Last night...My gran...Squashed hedgehog on her head...'

Miss Proudfoot stamped her feet again. 'No more stories please. We all know your gran is a charming lady who would never do anything to hurt a poor little hedgehog. And I think you had

58

better stay in at lunch-time, Verity. You've still got last night's homework to do. I saw your Maths work card inside your desk.'

So while the other children roared around the playing field or played 'Snap' in the bike shed, Verity sat at her desk and chased numbers round her page. If it took five boys three days to paint the school hall, and six girls two days to wash the graffiti off the staffroom door, how long would it take ten parents to mend the hole in the PE shed roof?

'How do I know?' grumbled Verity. 'I don't even care.'

She opened her desk and took out her box. Soundlessly, she lifted out the brown bag and untied the silky ribbons. The sweets glowed. Temptingly.

'All right, then. I'll show them. I'll tell the truth all afternoon and see how they like it,' she said to herself. 'I'll eat the biggest one I can see. And then I'll tell Emily Forthright she's got a big mouth, and I'll tell Donna she's got a big nose, and I'll tell Miss Proudfoot all about the 'Snap' games, and then they'll all be sorry. Serve them right too.'

Her hand dived into the bag. A bony set of fingers clamped over it. She looked up into the

jubilant face of Miss Proudfoot.

'So, Verity the truth teller. I might have known.'
She released Verity's wrist, then seized the bag and
dangled it by its ribbons. 'There's only one way to
deal with greedy children who eat sweets in class.
Isn't there?'

Verity shuddered all over. 'Oh no, miss. You
can't. Not today. Not when there's an important
visitor…'

But Miss Proudfoot was already marching down
to the teacher's table. Outside a bell clanged, and
the children came streaming back into the room,

squabbling and fighting just for the fun of it.

'Silence,' pleaded Miss Proudfoot. 'Sit down, everyone. Sit up. Look this way.'

Verity buried her head in her hands. Hidden in her palm was one small blue lozenge. All the rest were sitting on the class register, far, far away.

'Before we begin,' Miss Proudfoot announced. 'I am pleased to tell you that Verity has most kindly brought a bag of humbugs to share with us all. Isn't that generous of her?'

Heads nodded, eyebrows jiggled, and Miss Proudfoot danced round the room making sure she visited every single seat. The children gaped at the beautiful sweets in wonder and sniffed at them curiously. Lavender? Melted butter? Chocolate and peaches? Whatever the scent was, it promised to taste unimaginable. Mouths watered, lips opened, eyes rolled. Miss Proudfoot chose a sparkling sweet for herself, then plumped the bag back on her register. The whole class sighed.

Verity sighed loudest of all, and stowed her own lozenge deep inside her skirt pocket.

At that moment, the classroom door opened and the headmaster came in, followed by a crowd of clicking photographers, a team of scribbling reporters, and a large blustering man in a bow tie.

'Mr Samson Smirkalot. Our very own Town Mayor,' bellowed the head. 'He's come to take a look at our school.'

'A last look,' shouted a voice which appeared to come from Emily Forthright's direction. 'My dad says old Smirkface wants to pull it down. He says old Spoutalot ought to…' The lozenges were beginning to work.

'Yes, yes.' The head gave a squeaky laugh and signalled at Miss Proudfoot to remove the appalling little beast. 'As I was telling you, children, Mr Smirkalot has all sorts of exciting plans for our future…'

'And all of them rotten ones,' interrupted someone from the nature corner. Could it be Peter, or Jake? 'He wants to turn our whole village into a car-park, you know.'

'That's right,' agreed Miss Proudfoot, who had finished her sweet and was now giving Emily Forthright a gold star for honesty. 'And what's more, he's going to make lots of money out of it. So he'll be rich, and we'll all be homeless.' With that, she broke down in tears.

The card players patted her shoulders comfortingly.

'Never mind, miss,' said Donna. 'We'll make

sure he doesn't get away with it. Won't we, gang?'

The whole class, with the exception of Verity, stood up and cheered. Then they turned to face Mr Smirkalot and booed. The press reporters scribbled and the photographers clicked. This was the best day of their lives. School visits were usually incredibly boring.

'Ha, ha, ha!' The head laughed again, but more pathetically. 'Just our little joke, Mr Mayor. I'm sure you understand. Youthful high spirits and all that sort of thing.'

This was a nightmare. Children should be seen and not heard. Everyone knew that. They should keep their thoughts to themselves and never, never offend a grown-up. Especially a very important grown-up like Samson Smirkalot. He had a big car. He was rich. He was powerful...

He was purple in the face and seemed to be choking on his bow tie. 'I, I, I...' he blustered. 'I, I, I...'

'Have a cough sweet, sir,' suggested one of the reporters, who wanted to know what he was trying to say. She stuck her hand in the brown bag on the teacher's table and popped a lozenge into the Mayor's open mouth.

He stopped spluttering. He squeezed his lips

together and sucked in his cheeks. He swallowed noisily. 'Delicious,' he murmured. 'Just the thing. Now, where was I?'

'Building a giant car-park,' prompted Emily.

'Flattening the village,' added Peter and Jake.

'Giving me the sack,' wailed Miss Proudfoot.

'Getting very rich,' finished Donna.

'Absolutely,' agreed Samson Smirkalot with a huge, happy smirk. Instead of rubbing his nose, he rubbed his palms together, as if he could already see the mountains of bank-notes. 'I'm going to flatten this dreary little dump out of existence and construct the country's first "Tarmac-Town" Theme Car-Park. I shall call it "Smirkalot's Expanding Spaces", and I'll be the wealthiest man in the whole of Europe.'

The news-reporters finished scribbling, and formed a rugby scrum in the classroom doorway as they headed off to use their car phones.

'And now,' Mr Smirkalot continued cheerfully, 'I think I'll go home. I've seen quite enough of this ghastly little school and its even ghastlier children. Goodbye to you all, and good riddance.'

And heaving the photographers out of his way, he opened the fire doors and skipped off across the playing field, humming an old pop song as he

went. 'Give me money…That's what I want…Tum
te tum…Money…What I want…'

The Headmaster watched Samson Smirkalot go, then slumped down in Miss Proudfoot's chair and began to moan quietly to himself.

Verity, who had been sitting with her eyes shut throughout all the commotion, slowly spread her fingers and peeped through the cracks. Miss Proudfoot seemed a new person.

'Well, I don't care what the rotten old Mayor does to the school,' she was saying, as she tipped the counting blocks on the floor and sat down to play with them. 'I'm fed up with being a teacher anyway. I hate adding up the dinner money, and I hate being sensible all the time. I'd much rather be something silly, like…'

She built a tall tower of red and yellow cubes, then knocked it over and giggled, '…like a ventriloquist with a monkey puppet. Or a fire eater. Or a juggler perhaps.'

She grabbed three oranges from the nature table and threw them wildly into the air so that they all fell in impossible places. Down the back of

the radiators, inside the light fittings, bouncing off the head's nose.

'Rubbish!' shouted the children joyfully. 'Miss Proudfoot can't catch for toffee.' To prove it, they all raided the nature display and hurled fruit at each other.

I don't believe this, thought Verity. All my favourite stories are coming true. The bank robber, the gorilla, the post van, the old lady. Even the juggling lessons. I just hope nobody decides to play Cowboys and…'

But someone had already remembered it was time for a Drama lesson.

'North American Indians,' shouted Jake above the racket. 'Would you like a game with us, Miss P? Seeing as you don't want to be a teacher any more.'

'No, miss,' warned Verity. 'Don't do it. They'll…'

'Ooooh, yes please,' Miss Proudfoot kicked her plastic cubes out of the way and followed the children as they whooped and bounded out of the

fire doors towards the goalposts.

'Aren't you going to join them?' The head stood up wearily and leaned his forehead against the window. The children were tying Miss Proudfoot to one of the posts, and dancing round her waving invisible hatchets.

'No thanks,' said Verity. 'I don't seem to feel very well. I think I'll just do some work till home-time instead.' She opened her desk and took out her maths card, note book and pencils. 'Sir,' she added, when the head had finished wiping his eyes. 'You know what you told us in assembly yesterday, about never telling lies?'

He nodded weakly.

'Well. Are you still sure about that? I mean, you wanted us to be polite to the Mayor this afternoon, didn't you? And that would have been a fib, because we all think he's mean and greedy. So is it always best to be honest? Is it really that simple?'

'Aaaahhh.' The headmaster patted his brows on his damp hanky so that his bald patch shone. He seemed to have forgotten the question.

'Only, it seems to me,' Verity went on helpfully, 'perhaps it's sometimes better if people try to say the *right* thing, even if it's not exactly true.'

The head groaned. This was all too much. He

staggered across to the teacher's table and absent-mindedly fumbled in the brown bag until he found a nice big sweet. Then he munched it noisily, like a small boy with a mouthful of thumb. 'In what way?' he managed to ask between gulps.

'Oh. You know.' Verity carefully removed her christening present from the register, put it back in its box and stowed it inside her schoolbag. 'For instance…Last night my Gran asked me what I thought of her new hat, so I said it was horrible and she was really upset.' She shrugged. This wasn't at all easy. 'And now I think it would have been kinder to say it looked lovely.'

'Nonsense,' the head roared, swallowing the last sliver of blue sugar. He stretched his mouth so widely that Verity could see the sparkling spots on his tongue. 'If you told her that, she'd wear it in the street and everyone would laugh at her.'

'Mmmm.' Verity frowned. 'But what about poor Mr Smirkalot? Won't he get thrown out of the Town Hall now? All because we told the truth about him.'

'Who cares?' The headmaster thumped his hand on the table so hard he bruised himself and had to blow on his knuckles. 'Serves him jolly well right. It was about time someone wiped the smirk off his fat face. It's a pity no one said what they really thought about him years ago.'

The door flew open, and before Verity could think of an answer, one of the reporters from the local TV station gave a 'Cooee'.

'Excuse me, Mr Headmaster,' she said, pulling a cassette recorder out of her bag. 'But do you think I could have a word or two about these closure plans? We'd love a short interview for tonight's *News and Views* show.'

'Certainly, m'dear.' The head thumped his other hand on the table and winced. 'It'll be a pleasure. Ask away.'

The girl led him out of the room, and Verity was left alone.

Outside, the children had finished their Apache Sundance game, and were calling each other rude names. The sort of things they were normally far too well mannered to say. 'Drippy-nose', and 'Pimply-knees', and 'Cabbage-head.' And worse.

Two of the boys were rolling on the ground, stuffing grass cuttings down one another's collars, while the class bully was being chased across the field by a hoard of screaming girls. He looked terrified, and he seemed to be crying.

Miss Proudfoot, who had escaped from the

goalpost by untying the knots with her teeth, was now climbing up the school drain-pipe. 'I'm going to find all the lost tennis balls and do my juggling act on the classroom roof,' she was yelling. But no one was listening. Not even Verity.

She had packed her books away, stacked her chair neatly on her desk, and lined herself up at the door. She looked at her watch. Five, four, three, two, one... The bell rang for home-time, and she hurried away down the corridor to reach the real world, where people still enjoyed telling a few fibs now and again.

She hurtled along the pavement until she came to the post office, where she collapsed on the iron bench to get her breath back.

SHOCK! HORROR! read the newspaper hoardings. 'Local politician tells the truth. Village to be flattened. Smirkalot spills the beans.'

'So there you are at last. I've been searching for you everywhere. Twice round Jupiter, and three times through the Milky Way.'

Verity jumped to her feet in surprise as the thin voice crackled down her ear. She span on her heels and sat down again, just in time to see the old lady appear on the bench beside her. 'Please don't give me any more of your christening presents,'

Verity begged. 'I've had quite enough trouble with this one…'

A bony finger waggled in front of her nose to silence her. 'You think you've got problems? What about me? There's been a terrible to-do at headquarters. Apparently I broke the unwritten rule…"No magic unless – she's a royal princess". Although, how I was expected to know about that if no one could be bothered to write it down, I really don't understand.'

She tapped a spiky nail on Verity's shoulder. 'Anyway, I shouldn't have given you the spell, and that's that. Dangerous stuff in the wrong hands, or so I'm told. You didn't eat many of the lozenges, did you?'

'Oh no,' said Verity honestly. 'In fact, I only tried one. But…'

'Doesn't matter,' the old lady chuckled. 'It's a bottomless bag, you know. Supposed to last a lifetime, if you can believe what the salesman told me.'

She held out her crinkled hands, and Verity drew the lop-sided box from her schoolbag as fast as she could.

'Here you are,' she said. 'To tell you the truth, I'm really glad to get rid of it.'

'Oh yes?' The old lady cackled for no obvious reason, then stood up to hide the gift amongst the dark folds of her hem.

'Shall I ever see you again?' asked Verity, not sure whether she wanted to or not.

'All depends.' The voice was fading already. Verity could see the shape of the bench through the swirling black skirt. 'If you marry a prince when you grow up, and if you happen to have a baby girl called Veri…' The old lady was gone.

'I can promise you this,' whispered Verity to the

post-box. 'If I ever meet a prince, I'm going to run a mile. And I'm certainly never going to kiss any talking frogs.'

Verity crept indoors and went up to her bedroom. She thought it best to keep out of everyone's way until tea-time, so she sprawled on her bed and opened her English homework book.

'Remember the Headmaster's assembly this week,' it said. 'Now tell a story in your own words. The title is, "Telling The Truth".'

Verity chewed her pen. She scratched her ears. She walked up and down. She went to the bathroom and cleaned her teeth. Twice. She had a fight with her pillow, and let it win. By the time Mum called her, she had only written two lines.

'Hurry up,' Mum was shouting. 'Come and see who's on TV. I think it's one of your teachers.'

Verity picked up her book and ran downstairs. *News and Views* had just started in the living-room, and her headmaster's face filled the screen.

Above a background of shrieks and whoops and screams, he was saying, 'To be perfectly honest, I'd like to punch that Smirkalot fellow right on the nose. But luckily for him, I'm not that sort of a

person.'

'So what *do* you intend to do?' asked the reporter earnestly.

'Force him to resign, of course.' The headmaster was about to thump his hand on the table, but he changed his mind. Both his fists were wrapped in bandages. 'If everyone in the village stands together, he won't have a chance. We can beat him easily. After all, he's already admitted he's only in it for the money. You all heard him. He can't deny it.'

The picture changed, and this time Samson Smirkalot appeared. He was still smirking, so the effects of the truth lozenge couldn't have worn off yet.

'Don't want to deny it,' he boasted, sticking out his tongue. It was covered in spots. 'I want to be rich. I've always wanted to be rich. I want to buy myself a lovely big house, with a…' He leaned forwards, smirking even wider. 'Do you want to know what I'd really like?'

The reporter nodded, so he went on.

'I'd like a circus of my very own. That's all I've ever really wanted. I don't want to be Mayor. I don't want to wear a smart suit and work in an office all day. I want to be a Ringmaster, and have lots of clowns and acrobats and jugglers…' He tailed off dreamily. Somehow, he didn't seem quite so wicked any more.

'I see,' said the reporter, although she obviously didn't. 'But tell me…' She paused. Someone had just handed her a sheet of paper. She read it quickly, then passed it to Mr Smirkalot.

'News Flash,' she announced to the camera. 'Giant car-park deal off. Town Mayor, Samson Smirkalot, sacked from the council. Local village saved from the cement mixers.'

The item switched to a view of the school, where a tiny Miss Proudfoot could just be seen, juggling triumphantly on the PE shed roof. 'Easy peasy,' she seemed to be yelling.

Mum picked up the zapper and turned the programme off. 'Thank goodness for that,' she said. 'All's well that ends well. Is that your gran I can hear ringing the bell?'

'Don't know,' Verity began. 'I can't see through walls…'

'Verity!' gargled Mum. 'Watch your tongue.'

'OK,' said Verity. 'I know. I mustn't tell stories and I mustn't tell the truth. But it's all getting very confusing.' And she scurried away to open the front door.

Gran came in wearing a long red cardigan, a pair of flappy trousers, and an extremely starchy expression. 'If you've got anything to say about my new outfit, I don't want to hear it,' she said, plonking herself on the settee. She looked awful. Nothing fitted. Everything was too bright, or too baggy, or too...

'I don't care what you wear,' said Verity warmly. She sat down next to Gran and wriggled as close as she dared. 'You always look lovely to me.'

Gran unstiffened like a thawed-out slice of frozen bread and gave Verity a hug that smelled of apple scones. 'If I'm absolutely honest,' she said, 'that pink hat was a terrible mistake. I shouldn't have bought it in the first place, but I can never resist a bargain.'

She gave Verity a second hug. 'That's better,' she said with a smile. 'All forgiven. Now tell me one of your funny stories. What did you do at school today?'

'Oh, nothing much.' Verity's mouth had gone dry. 'Tidied our desks. Stayed in at lunch-time to

catch up on my homework. Did some sums in the afternoon.'

Gran's face dropped. 'Is that all? No Red Indians? No war dances? No jokes about Miss Proudfoot?'

'Don't encourage her, Gran,' said Mum. 'She talks far too much nonsense as it is.'

'Too true,' grumbled Bill, stumping in and giving Gran a peck on the cheek. 'She tells too many tales as well.'

'I'm sorry, Bill.' Verity looked so genuinely

upset that he almost forgot to frown. 'I didn't mean to be rotten. I won't do it again.'

He gave her a friendly punch in the arm. To be fair, he hadn't got into any real trouble with Mum, so… 'All right, then. But watch yourself, kid. OK?'

'OK.' Verity began to relax. Mum was painting her nails, and Bill had gone upstairs to wash his hair. She leaned comfortably against Gran and sighed happily.

'Want to help me butter some scones?' asked Gran.

'You bet,' said Verity. And they both trooped out to the kitchen.

'You know,' said Gran as the kettle boiled merrily. 'I'd really love to tell that nosy Mrs Grummet what I think of her. She's bought a hat exactly the same as mine, and she looks just like a pink hedgehog.'

'Would you really, Gran? Are you sure?' Verity grinned. She delved into her skirt pocket and fished out the last blue lozenge. It was a bit fluffy, but otherwise it seemed as sparkly as ever. 'Try this,' she whispered. 'First thing tomorrow morning. But not before.'

'That's funny,' said Mum to herself, as she flicked through the English book Verity had left on the coffee table. 'I always thought that girl liked writing stories.'

Bill had just walked in with a towel wrapped round his head, so she held out the page for him to see. Underneath the title, in rather squiggly, old-fashioned writing were the following words: 'The Truth Is Rarely Pure And Never Simple'. That was all.

'Very interesting, I'm sure,' said Bill. 'But there's a frog upstairs in the sink. And I think it's trying to tell me something.'

Which is the end of this story, more or less. Except to say that Verity soon found her imagination again, although she always thought long and hard before she used it, and when she grew up she became a writer of books. Some of them were full of amazing true facts, and some of them were full of adventures about gorillas and frogs and burglars in post vans. But she didn't marry a prince, and her children were never allowed to accept christening presents from strange old ladies.

As for Miss Proudfoot and Samson Smirkalot? They ran away together and joined the circus. Of course.

Also in Puffin

WAR BOY
Michael Foreman

Barbed wire and barrage balloons, gas masks and Anderson shelters, loud bangs and piercing whines – the sights and sounds of war were all too familiar to a young boy growing up in the 1940s.

Lowestoft, a quiet seaside town in Suffolk, was in the front line during World War Two. Bombing raids, fires and trips to the air-raid shelters became almost daily events for young Michael Foreman and his friends.

But gas masks were great for rude noises, gobstoppers were still good to suck and the Hill Green Gang could still try to beat the Ship Road Gang. Father Christmas would tell tales of his days as a cabin boy on the great clippers, the old tramp could spin a good yarn round the camp fire, and nothing could beat Mrs Ruthern's rabbit pie!

OUR KID
Ann Pilling

Frank has high hopes that the money from his paper round will solve all his problems, but the new job plunges him into another world. He meets Tim, with his rich family and his gorgeous sister Cass, and Sister Maggie at the convent (why, he wonders, do nuns read the *TV Times*?). Then there's Foxy, hanging about the streets at all hours.

Frank emerges from this warm and fascinating novel with a new view of his slob of a big brother, his lonely dad, and Foxy, the cat burglar, and discovers 'the amazing things people will do for love.'

WOLF

Gillian Cross

Cassy has never understood the connection between the secret midnight visitor to her nan's flat and her sudden trips to stay with her mother. But this time it seems different. She finds her mother living in a squat with her boyfriend Lyall and his son Robert. Lyall has devised a theatrical event for children on wolves, and Cassy is soon deeply involved in presenting it. Perhaps too involved – for she begins to sense a very real and terrifying wolf stalking her.

THE OUTSIDE CHILD

Nina Bawden

Imagine suddenly discovering you have a step-brother and -sister no one has ever told you about! It's the most exciting thing that's ever happened to Jane, and she can't wait to meet them. Perhaps at last she will become part of a 'proper' family, instead of for ever being the outside child. So begins a long search for her brother and sister, but when she finally does track them down, Jane finds there are still more surprises in store!

THE FOX OF SKELLAND

Rachel Dixon

Samantha's never liked the old custom of Foxing Day – the fox costume especially gives her the creeps. So when Jason and Rib, children of the new publicans at The Fox and Lady, find the costume and Jason wears it to the fancy-dress disco, she's sure something awful will happen.

Then Sam's old friend Joseph sees the ghost of the Lady and her fox. Has she really come back to exact vengeance on the village? Or has her appearance got something to do with the spate of burglaries in the area?

ESIO TROT
Roald Dahl

Mr Hoppy is in love with Mrs Silver. But Mrs Silver has eyes only for Alfie, her pet tortoise. How can he ever compete with such a rival? He comes up with a bold plan to win his lady's love, involving some clever riddles and a whole army of tortoises. Will Mr Hoppy's patience be rewarded? And what's to become of Alfie?

A highly comic and unusual love story.

JUST FERRET
Gene Kemp

Owen Hardacre, otherwise known as Ferret, has been dragged around the country by his artist father and been to so many schools that he doesn't expect much from Cricklepit Combined School. But when he makes friends with Beany and Minty and gains the respect of Sir, things begin looking up . . . even the reading!

Meet Ferret, his friends *and* enemies in this fifth story of the pupils of Cricklepit Combined School.

DID YOU THINK I WOULD LEAVE YOU CRYING?
Moira Miller

This collection of sensitive and moving stories traces the effects of conflict and compassion across the years; the friendship, the heroism and the cruelty of war.

RT, MARGARET AND THE RATS OF NIMH
Jane Leslie Conly

When Margaret and her brother RT get lost in the forests surrounding Thorn Valley, help comes from an unexpected quarter when the super-rats of NIMH come to their rescue. Margaret and RT must return home before winter sets in, but the incredible events of their summer in the valley become the biggest secret they have ever had to keep.

The third thrilling story in this classic trilogy about the rats of NIMH.

ONLY MIRANDA
Tessa Krailing

A new town, a tiny flat over the Chinese takeaway, a new school mid-term and a place next to Chrissie Simpson, the most unpopular girl in the class. Things aren't looking great for Miranda. But her father has gone to prison and this at least is a chance of a new life for her and her mother. Miranda bounces back in true style: she befriends poor Chrissie and when the dinner money is stolen and Chrissie is suspected, Miranda is determined to prove her innocence.

TWIN AND SUPER TWIN
Gillian Cross

Ben, David and Mitch had only meant to start the Wellington Street Gang's bonfire, not blow up all their fireworks as well. But even worse is what happens to David's arm in the process. Until, that is, they realize that this extraordinary event could be very useful in their battles with the Wellington Street Gang.

WHO IS FRANCES RAIN?
Margaret Buffie

It's going to be a long hot summer for Lizzie. This year the whole happy family, including her mother's new husband, are going to stay with her grandmother on the lake, usually the highlight of the summer. She decides to get away from everyone and all their bickering, goes exploring by herself and makes a few discoveries which make this summer more exciting and memorable than any other.

THE SECRET IN MIRANDA'S WARDROBE
Sheila Greenwald

Miranda is a solitary child, but her mother is outrageous and always out socialising. When Miranda finds a beautiful old doll she turns her wardrobe into a secret home for it, and gains confidence through playing with the doll – and her lonely life begins to change.

TIMEPIECES
David Leney

A cycle of stories – one for each month – about the lives of contemporary people, young and old, in a small Suffolk village. A strong sense of the passing years emerges, giving a delightful insight into the dramas enacted by the various children and their families. There is the race between two boys to find a missing tortoise, a family's stay in a beautiful country house only to discover that it is not the earthly paradise they had supposed, a story about conker fights and bullies, the death of a family pet, a disastrous school trip and an amusing misunderstanding over a dead man's wellington boots.